Steve Trost

About the Poet

ERIKA MEITNER is the author of *Inventory at the All-night Drugstore*, winner of the 2002 Anhinga Prize for Poetry. Her poems have been anthologized widely and have appeared in publications, including *The New Republic*, *Virginia Quarterly Review*, *The American Poetry Review*, and on Slate.com. She is an assistant professor of English at Virginia Tech, and is also completing her doctorate in religious studies at the University of Virginia.

IdEAL CiTiES

The National Poetry Series was established in 1978 to ensure the publication of five poetry books annually through five participating publishers. Publication is funded by the Lannan Foundation, Stephen Graham, the Joyce & Seward Johnson Foundation, Glenn & Renee Schaeffer, and the Juliet Lea Hillman Simonds Foundation.

2009 Competition Winners

Julie Carr of Denver, Colorado, *Sarah — Of Fragments and Lines*
Chosen by Eileen Myles, to be published by Coffee House Press

Colin Cheney of Brooklyn, New York, *Here Be Monsters*
Chosen by David Wojahn, to be published by University of Georgia Press

Carrie Fountain of Austin, Texas, *Burn Lake*
Chosen by Natasha Trethewey, to be published by Penguin Books

Erika Meitner of Blacksburg, Virginia, *Ideal Cities*
Chosen by Paul Guest, to be published by HarperCollins Publishers

Jena Osman of Philadelphia, Pennsylvania, *The Network*
Chosen by Prageeta Sharma, to be published by Fence Books

Also by Erika Meitner

Inventory at the All-night Drugstore

C.1

IdEAL CiTiES

poems

Erika Meitner

HARPER PERENNIAL

NEW YORK • LONDON • TORONTO • SYDNEY • NEW DELHI • AUCKLAND

HARPER ● PERENNIAL

HarperCollins books may be purchased for educational, business, or sales promotional use. For information, please write: Special Markets Department, HarperCollins Publishers, 10 East 53rd Street, New York, NY 10022.

FIRST EDITION

Designed by Joy O'Meara

Library of Congress Cataloging-in-Publication Data is available upon request.

ISBN 978-0-06-199518-7

10 11 12 13 14   ID/RRD   10 9 8 7 6 5 4 3 2 1

for Steve and Oz

————

and for Frances Zimmerman, Z"L

(1913–2008)

The new monuments are made of artificial materials,
plastic, chrome, and electric light.

—Robert Smithson,
"Entropy and the New Monuments" (1966)

———

I am a wall
and my breasts are towers.
But for my lover I am
a city of peace.

—*The Song of Songs: A New Translation*
(translated by Ariel and Chana Bloch)

Contents

Part Two: *Ideal Cities*

Acknowledgments

Grateful acknowledgment goes to the editors of the following journals and anthologies where these poems, sometimes in different form, first appeared:

32 Poems: "You Are Invisible"
The American Poetry Review: "The Violent Legacy of Household Monogamy," "Christmas Towns," "In Dispraise of Heat"
Anti-: "January Towns"
Barn Owl Review: "Preventing Teen Cough Medicine Abuse," "In Praise of Heat"
Blackbird: "The Upstairs Notebook"
Cavalier Literary Couture: "O Edinburgh"
Cave Wall: "Schools of Prophetic Interpretation"
Diode: "Poem With/out a Face"
The Florida Review: "Miracle Blanket"
Indiana Review: "Pediatric Eschatology"
Iron Horse Literary Review: "May the World to Come Be Neon, Be Water"
The Journal: "North Slope Borough"
The New Republic: "Ideal Cities"

Nextbook.org: "North Country Canzone," "Pharaoh's Daughter"
Prairie Schooner: "1944," "The Chimneys in New Jersey,"
Redivider: "Interstate Cities"
Shenandoah: "Massive Destruction"
Slate.com: "Vinyl-Sided Epiphany"
The Southeast Review: "In the Passport Line"
The Southern Review: "Careful"
Virginia Quarterly Review: "Elegy with Construction Sounds, Water, Fish"
Washington Square: "As Boys Grow (1957)," "Godspeed"
Whiskey Island: "We Need to Make Mute Things," "Wound Laced with Evening News, in Which Criss Angel Appears and Vanishes"

"Slinky Dirt with Development Hat" first appeared on the blog Starting Today: Poems for the First 100 Days (100dayspoems.blogspot.com), posted March 5, 2009, and has been reprinted in *Starting Today: 100 Poems for Obama's First 100 Days*, edited by Rachel Zucker and Arielle Greenberg, University of Iowa Press, 2010.

Many thanks to the Blue Mountain Center, and the Virginia Center for the Creative Arts, where lots of these poems were completed. I am also indebted to my virtual NaPoWriMo group for their presence, encouragement, talent, and tenacity: Sandra Beasley, Mary Biddinger, Oliver de la Paz, and Aimee Nezhukumatathil. Special thanks to Melissa Cocci Luckett for D.C. baby-related sanity, Taije Silverman and David Stack for their editorial expertise, and Kim Beck for her artistic inspiration and title. And my gratitude goes to Paul Guest, the National Poetry Series, and the fine folks at Harper Perennial—especially Michael Signorelli.

This book wouldn't exist without Steve Trost; he helped most.

part one

Rental
Towns

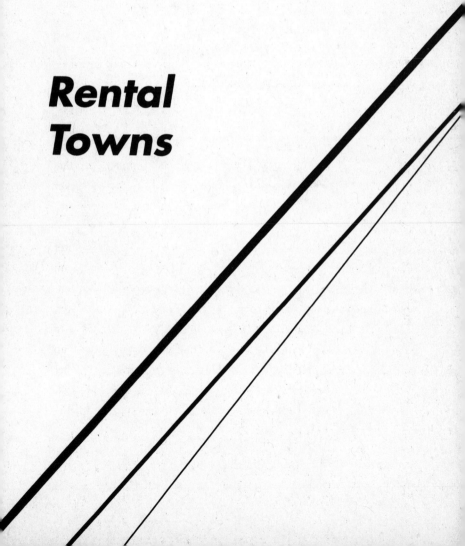

North Slope Borough

My heart is an Alaskan fishing village during whaling season,
which is to say that everyone is down by the thawing sea.
The huts on stilts are empty, and my heart is a harpoon,
a homemade velveteen parka, hood lined with wolverine.
My mouth has no zipper, which helps me remember
how to say O. O I miss home. When I close my eyes,
I see the F train's twin headlights blooming into the station.
When I close my eyes, its warm wind sweeps hair from my face,
the way my grandmother did with her hands, to see my eyes.
Home is the place with plastic slipcovers on the couch.
Home is the place with heavy brown shoes misaligned at the door.
When I close my eyes, I look for an entryway into the earth.
I dream of a porcupine, though I can't recall if I've ever seen one.
I dream of my dead friend, who has no voice, but tells me to slow down.
We walk together to the neighborhood bar. It is summer. It is night.
I have no choice. In my dream, my dead friend gives me a fish.
I roll it up like a newspaper. I put a toothpick in it and we walk slowly
to Brooklyn. My words don't mean anything, because right now
my son is coughing in another room. I can hear him through the walls.
He sits up in his crib and waits for me. The world is a hollow
white door; when I close my eyes, it spins like a dime on tile.
It spins like something gentle knocked off a table. One day,
my heart will ascend from the subway tunnel. It will burst
into sunlight past the Court Street Station. My heart is a chainsaw,
an awl boring through leather. My heart is old-school graffiti—

a tag that zigs on metal, gets applause when it pulls into the station—
it's that uplifting. Some days the world is too lonely. My heart
wants to play chess with another heart inside my body.

Vinyl-Sided Epiphany

The windows on the soon-to-be luxury
condos across the way say things
to the darkness I can't hear. Sometimes
they're blocked by the train masticating
its way across town. Now and then

I can interpret their blank banter,
reminiscent of that ribbon gymnastics
no one ever watches during the Olympics.
They gracefully signal about our frugality (fragility),
a howling yard dog (not ours) and the rain

like a strange barrage of so many shot marbles.
The bullets we thought were firecrackers
turned out to be bullets. I take the trash out
vinyl nights crippled with fear that thumps
home from work at 3 a.m. We finally decide

to take a break after the well-meaning Block
Association gives out rolls of clear trash bags
in the hopes we'd pick up after the dealers
and delinquents who chuck Sprite bottles from
car windows or drop chicken boxes at the curb.

Yes, we'll ride off and leave the neighbor's voice
through the floor, rusty, molten, like pouring

pennies in a jar (that metallic taste, that exact
heaviness). You didn't specify how long we'd abandon
those tiny teacups, closet of hats, the meat grinder

attached to the side of the counter. We'd be safe
while someone else inherited our condiments.
But the rest stops would be anonymous, highway
industrial and rutted. I'd have to learn
new ways to eavesdrop on the neighbors,

on the rain, on us—on the same night lined
with an old bath mat that stretches everywhere.
We spackle small wall-holes with toothpaste
and apprehension, erase all visible traces,
though we're still as obvious as my student

who plays the ukulele and is no longer my student;
he sent me a broken-heart poem after his girlfriend
dumped him which used broken things as similes
for his heart. *For now*, she said in his poem—
that's how long they were apart.

We Need to Make Mute Things

I translate stories at the McDonald's, second floor:
Portrait of a Bus Line. What Makes People Laugh.
There is one about a psychological experiment that starts,
The crowd entered the concert hall. Everyone took their seats.
There is not one person who didn't take their seat.

The bathroom here is clean and I am waiting
for my tutor who is late and the McDonald's
pretends it's a river, looks out on an office building
covered in silver, a sculpture that simulates a wall
of undulating water. The cashiers of my pregnancy

have been telling me everything crucial: today Tina said
to bring a real pillow to the hospital to avoid their vinyl
and gave me a free milkshake with my McChicken. I am
cumbersome and forget my own girth, though in my winter coat
I blend with everyone else while I translate dumbed down

newspaper stories and truncated fables from Hebrew to English:
one on how babies learn language, and another about a poor man
who finds a coin on Shabbat that he's not allowed to pick up.
Even the metro donned a disguise to avoid the story
of the astronaut in love who drives miles in diapers.

On the way here, on the Orange line, Syria with his
gold-trimmed leather Bible told Desiree about Jesus

and a Chinese man got on for one stop to sing
Silent Night. The Rosslyn station is a long way up.
I am pregnant and the world is too noisy. Eventually

the sky will open and someone will gaze down on the earth.
The metro is hushed, covered in salt, honeycombed in cement.
I pretend I am Sputnik, unmanned, viable, perfectly round
and hiccuping. Orbiting. I would like to pass this exam.
I have two hearts, and the second one beats faster. I can hear it

weekly on a Doppler scope on the left side more strongly though
we need to make mute things the world is too noisy
the faster the heart the more I can translate the noise
of the train and the doors opening then everyone
took their seats and so did we.

Kick Me

When they hired me via phone I drove my Honda cross-country
and moved into a cottage off Highway 1 that belonged
to a minimalist anthropologist on sabbatical: television set hidden in
the closet, chairs made of driftwood, no chemicals allowed
for cleaning but vinegar and sea salt. I kept expecting to wake up
somewhere less bizarre and gorgeous, but I was in Santa Cruz:
dreadlocked ten-year-olds riding bicycles while balancing
surfboards under one arm, lemon trees in the yard, the Pacific
rolling along cliffs like a glossy vacation postcard
sent from the place where even God retires.

My cottage was tucked behind a stretch of all-night falafel joints,
and drive-thru espresso huts. The butchers at Esperanza Market
grilled skewered chickens on poles in metal half-barrels
stationed on the sidewalk like mini-tanks, smoke drifting
in my window Saturdays, making me so hungry I'd walk right past
the health food store, its sign engineered by anarchist employees
as a weekly font of motivation: "Subvert the Dominant Paradigm"
above "VitaPro Sale—Entire Line $6.99!" I didn't know anyone
in town then, and on days when I wasn't teaching, cashiers
at the Food & Herb Bin were my only social interaction. Everything

seemed equally symbolic to me that year, "Sign here"
and "Receipt in the bag?" taking on as much weight
as the kid who stood next to those chickens each week
wearing a cardboard box with armholes cut out.

Someone had painted CAR WASH alongside an orange →
on his front; someone (else?) had sprayed KICK ME on his back
in the same fluorescent paint. He must have known this.
His arrow pointed to four boys hanging out in the parking lot
with crumpled newspaper rags and another with a hose—
weekend fundraiser for some unclear cause.

I often went to that market though they didn't take credit cards,
I was always short of cash, didn't speak any Spanish
and couldn't identify a full half of the produce—
weird green fruit like puckered mouths, another I later learned
was a local, über-sweet hybrid called pluot—
two-thirds plum, one-third apricot, varietals named
like lipstick: Red Ray, Dapple Dandy, and Flavor Heart,
along with the more ominous Hand Grenade and Last Chance,
which is what the Kick Me kid yelled late-afternoons
while he motioned cars toward the empty lot

and joyfully conducted an orchestra of traffic, danced in synch
to the the walk light's sound for the blind, and danced harder
when a man in a butcher's apron took the crisped chickens
back into the market, weaving under the meat's weight
like he was about to take a drunken swing at one of the piñatas
swaying in the window, candy carcasses filled with the best birthday
party potential—not the generic donkeys at white kids' parties.
These were premium Mexican TV mice, Spongebob Squarepants,
all three Powerpuff Girls suspended in mid-flight, and I wanted one
though I had no one to invite over, blindfold, spin around.

Instead of a piñata, I got a Bingo set that taught cartoon
Spanish: *pirata*, *bola*, *estrella*, and the most benevolent
glass-cupped saint candle on the shelf: Angel de la Guardia
in her white robe, eyes closed, single star over her feathered wings
unfurling in the printed darkness to shield a small girl
clutching a smaller boy. Arms raised like the most ethereal
school crossing-guard in a moment of divine rapture, this angel
channeled the best ecstasy and fearlessness, like the hippie rave girl
who got on the #26 bus barefoot in a patchwork skirt
with glitter-trimmed wings strapped to her back, to bless us all.

Each night before bed I lit that candle, which trailed gray smoke
down the hall of my bungalow, smoothing cars quiet, lulling
the whole unfamiliar neighborhood asleep—even the content cat
on a string in the neighbor's garden curled up snoozing on the stoop,
protected by the trip-wires of spiderwebs in the hedges—
while I was insomniac, listening to past-midnight radio mariachi
oompahing along, waiting for each new day to break
through the thick morning fog: a gleeful boy labeled KICK ME,
every angel sighting synchronicity, each stranger
I hadn't met yet an intact piñata dancing on its string.

Preventing Teen Cough Medicine Abuse

the poem I started with you in a motel
plateaued the poem I started with you

in a motel started spending evenings
at home with a rapid heartbeat we were not

in a motel the poem was in that place
with my hair draped across your chest

and something was wet it was unclear
what did I mention there was a rapid

heartbeat there was a raw unfinished
form there was an out-of-body skittling

with distortions of color and sound,
which is to say that you were

so beautiful in those dangerous
side effects that I couldn't

help it there were no programs
I couldn't help it no matter

how many pamphlets I couldn't
help it could be abused the

combination we left the bedspread
on I just (dextromethorphan) swooned

Small, Generic Night Towns

we stumbled all the way to your place—
sultry footpath of August
(snapped heels   busted straps)

—past the gas station that sold
underage cigarettes because
someone's mother didn't care

once

after last call, the air
couldn't hold any more lust we were
dizzy with the opposite of remorse and pretending
to converse   *(let's*

cross the threshold   to forgetfulness)

        (these keys are hard to push)

(shhhhh)

        swollen door; holding
        pattern; night like a terrarium;

your neighbor with a pair of dice tattooed on his arm out combing
the block for his cat named Chance who had vanished, have we
seen him, he asks

      among the spent firecracker
      casings? in the cluster of moths
      trailing yellow light?

      it doesn't seem like an accident
      that summer is always gin-soaked
      and static with

hush-hush wishes and
furtive sadness of

night growing
larger than us

holding its breath
for things gone
missing; holding
its breath for
too long

Poem With/out a Face

(after the photograph series *Marine Wedding* by Nina Berman)

Somewhere cadets are fed up
with polishing their shoes.
Not here. They eat chicken
in their special mess hall
and do chin-ups outside
my office window. Are they
ever deployed? The boy
without a face marries
his high school sweetheart
in Illinois. On their wedding day
the photographer was not
saddened by the resolve
in her face, or his lack of
ears, nose, chin. There is no
work for him because he has
no hands, so his bride
is a barkeep, serves Bud Dry
in plastic cups at a place
for locals. The cadets here
cadence call on the quad,
shimmy on their elbows
toward the Dean's trailer
as if they're receiving
incoming fire, but they're not,
and the photographer knows

we can read her photo
of the newlyweds any way
we want. Desire is serendipity,
is pity, is blind, is danger, is not
obligation, is poking the most
alien thing with a stick to see
if it stirs and clings, the way
a literary agent I slept with
one August after we got high
on a Brooklyn rooftop admitted,
when I woke up tucked
into hospital-corner sheets,
that he had attended a military
institute and could assemble
a rifle in less than thirty seconds
without light, which is to say
that unlike the bus security guard
I slept with in Israel who kept
his gun under the mattress and
told me nothing about anything
except for one childhood story
about a river in South Africa
that I remember exactly what
both of their faces felt like
under my fingertips in the
dark or maybe I don't.

O Edinburgh

it was night & we were always drunk
        or it was day (gray day) & I'd buy
                boxes of clementines on my way
        from school & keep them outside
my window on the sill so they'd stay
        cool—O Edinburgh, where we'd
                mash ourselves together on that shelf
        of bed after you lined up shoes
to toss, one by one, at the heater
        on the wall—open coils that glowed
                orange for 15-minute increments
        like a toaster, & when you'd hit
the button your shoes would thud
        like large fish tails slapping the sides
                of a boat & we rose with the wind's
        current, its November brogue, &
O Edinburgh, it spoke in tongues,
        flapped doors open & shut, howled
                until I couldn't remember exactly
        what happened in the dark except
that we curled ourselves up into
        the smallest specks until I wept
                over a horoscope & someone else's
        tattoo & I never loved you because
I was a wall of a city I had never been to

Another Experiment with Dissolving

A softball pounding a catcher's mitt,
the smell of rawhide and rough halves
squeezed together around a caught moment;
one summer gnat in the eye and my mitt
became a face-mask in the outfield
where I stood all summer with the bees
that don't sting orbiting the purple clover
and my sneakers, dipping and circling
the way the older girls flirted with boys
from the camp across the lake who wore
fresh plaid shirts when they were allowed to see us.

Sometimes there's a breaking open, Wendy explained
late one night with the counselor on the porch,
out of earshot. I thought of science class—
the egg entering a bottle's neck with a plump
after a match is lit and tossed into the glass
to erase all the oxygen. I didn't believe her
until Jon Bernstein tried an experiment
with surface tension behind the canteen.
I held my breath, and lowered the paper clip
to the surface. If your hand is steady enough,
something will dissolve a bit at a time.

This is not a test for acids, or a test for starch.
This is not another siphon experiment.

In the lake that summer I would tread water
for thirty straight minutes during free-swim
until I was breathless with my assigned buddy
in the deep end. During check, we shouted
our number, held up slick hands while our legs
worked like water wheels under the surface.
I was practicing for lifeguard training.
The final certification exam: to dive down
thirteen feet, push water back with my arms,
grab a rubber brick from the floor and raise it
to the sky. It took me nineteen tries, the water
near the bottom like the grip of a vise on
shop-class pine. The rising was easy
without the brick, with both arms carving
and digging to the surface. This is another

experiment with the skin of water. I was cut
with breath and couldn't stop thinking
of his face. Sometimes there was a fracture
open. There was music with test tubes,
and all of it was cacophonous because
after the experiment with the match,
I was the terrified remains in the lower bottle;
he was a wind vane, I was a ribbon
thermometer. We were an experiment
with two soda straws. We were buoyant
and exactly. We were why and how it works.

As Boys Grow (1957)

Inside this film, all the boys are shirtless.
Inside this film, a car's motion is internal.
The blank faces of the boys are pebbles.

Two boys in the grass repair a mower. They sit.
The summer sees them. There is a wet dream,
and last night, it spoke. It hangs in the air,
but does not talk assuredly in the light.

When a boy grows, his silence
splits and seizes inside the outfield.
It spreads out, possibly, and it wants.
It kicks; it talks with a stick
in autumn's lower parts.

The boys inside the locker room gather
in surroundings of the bench.
The coach removes his black baseball cap.
He talks of the dull season,
the hour of change. He talks.

He has a comfortable summary of the penis
complete on the board, bitter with chalk.
He is a wooden pointer.

The boys are gray hoods in bleachers,
are American cars, are knives
with one motion of their bodies.

Your body, the coach says from time to time.
Yet it is a mystery.

The boys compare inner gymnastics,
gather surroundings of who will snap off.
One proposes swim immediately before boiling up,
in order to see (together) an hour-oyster-pictograph.

The coach diagrams a head, which talks
when it is stimulated by a woman.

The fixed amount of up is the sun,
which waves inside an interpretive dance.
Something increases tenfold between their legs;
something else is exactly like a chicken egg.

The coach talks. His pencil kicks an ovary.
One boy refers to his portion of the baby.
His hand is wild.
A dot travels a tube.

The leading American knife
has one motion in the water
which talks to the car like that.

It is late.
Two boys are inside a skirt.
They want to go to the lagoon.
The girl is a bench.

In the book, something increases.
The girl falls and there is cake
and a swish; the hoof thing—it agrees.

On Saturday, in the adjacent waters,
after kicking, a boy hits one thing lightly.
The boy means it, in order to grow.

In Dispraise of Heat

The baby has a 104 fever this morning.
I pump him full of Motrin.
Our neighbor Ruth insists on cool washcloths.

She tells me to put them in his armpits.
She says she'll pray for him.
I say *thank you* though we're Jewish.

She means to ask Jesus for help on our behalf.
My friend from grade school died this week.
He had been missing four days before they found him in a subway.

His mother went to the Bronx one morning.
One morning like any other she went to identify his body.
I describe my son's fever to strangers.

I say he is *burning up*.
A woman leaves an iron on a white shirt.
She is subject to domestic distractions.

A woman smokes in bed and her cigarette slips.
While she dozes it lands on white sheets.
Her children are subject to unnecessary peril.

All the mothers give me advice.
There are alcohol baths, ice baths, alternating medications.
There are stories of undiagnosed pneumonia, of roseola.

But even my son's small bare feet are flushed with fever.
They fiddle with each other in his restless sleep.
My friend escaped from a locked psych ward.

My friend went out into the city.
There were sons huddled near office buildings.
There were sons busking for change in commuter stations.

When someone escapes like that, they call it *eloping*.
In grade school my father put a chain-link fire ladder under my bed.
Just in case, he said, so I thought right away of leaving.

But we will implement measures.
We will place cool hands on the foreheads of burning sons.
We will return them gently to bed.

A woman warms herself by a woodstove.
Her skirt shifts in the heat and it is nearly always fatal.
You can hear it in the whistle of the kettle.

Careful

Pyrex is supposed to be durable, but my husband assured me that
  anything
dropped from that height would shatter. My heart. It was utilitarian,
  that bowl,

and the tile was hard, but my arms were at arms' length. When my
  son rolled off
his changing table and plunged to the floor, he did not break like the
  Pyrex,

though his nose was bruised from carpet friction. I checked in on
  him every hour that night
to make sure he was still breathing, imagined invisible injuries that
  never materialized.

He dozed mightily in dinosaur pajamas, his small bare foot wedged
  between his crib bars.
When the Pyrex bowl shattered, it wasn't the same careful ache I
  felt when my father

broke the last of my antique juice glasses, which were actually
  irreplaceable. There was no
moment of sadness. I swept and vacuumed, got down on my knees
  to wipe the glittering

dust from the tiles, and thought, *unsafe*. The sharp edges on each
    piece were phonographs
that played small songs when their needles scratched my skin. My
    fingerprints became

road-trip karaoke, Muzak, though I couldn't shake every pit stop in
    West Virginia, no matter
the song on the radio—the clubfeet, oxygen tanks, the janitor at
    Burger King who told us

that all there was to do in that particular town was go fishing with
    his good-for-nothing sons.
The river was brown and swollen with rain. He was trying to close
    our section up to mop.

I wonder what the janitor catches, if he has a boat, if his job is a
    sinking down, or a rising up.
Pyrex used to be made from shock-resistant borosilicate glass. The
    vintage ads promised

marital bliss via gifts of transparent ovenware. My husband says
    people out West
are panning for gold again. Should we be shocked by this? In a river,
    gold tends to get stuck

in small rock crevices and wedged in pieces of wood. The last time
    we were out West,
all our photos vanished. The memory card got erased. We stayed in
    a bed and breakfast

in Utah where the owner had just lost his wife. We stayed in Hostel
    X. Gold is malleable,
ductile, impossible to fracture. One ounce can be drawn into a fifty-
    mile-long wire.

When we visited our new Hasidic neighbors, the wife told me, *thank
    G-d*, that she knew
there was a god because of all the bad things that might happen to
    her children that didn't.

She said this as she extracted a cherry pit from her year-old son's
    mouth. How he hadn't
choked was a mystery to me. She said this as her other sons dangled
    off the porch rails

and didn't fall. Before we had a child, we went out West and came
    back without pictures
of bison and unbroken prairie. Pyrex is no longer shock-resistant,
    and each thing we drop

reverts back to the earth—the pan with gold sediment that will not
    get melted into a half-
heart necklace, into a dangling charm shaped like a small child. My
    grandmother had

all three of us hanging on a chain, names engraved on the back. In
    streams, placer gold
is metal that's been weathered away from its motherlode, its original
    vein, sometimes by

a mining method called hushing. There is resilience and there is
    avoidance; there is a mother
shouting *careful* or *thank god* against the crippling fear that we will
    shatter and vanish. Hush.

Pediatric Eschatology

the nurse called back and told us to use bleach
on anything we touch, she said *wash everything*
in hot water, insisted *we won't treat you if*
you're asymptomatic, we won't, and made us
an appointment anyway. so we waited and waited
with the dog-eared magazines and recall posters
until someone in the waiting room asked if i knew
sweet jesus, and someone else told me a story
about their dentist and the rapture (this waiting room
was endless). there was no irony with that dentist
and i am obsessed with stale marshmallow peeps
and people who believe in the rapture—this idea
that they'll be sucked from their cars in the middle
of the day just saved from things like traffic. you can
learn many things about the rapture online:
that the rapture is again postponed, is difficult
to evaluate, is the falling away, is the only valid
hope, is your father's business of gathering, is
out of harmony with the doctrine of imminence,
is an instantaneous secret event, yet no one wrote
in the manual about what to do if your pediatrician's
office is in a methadone clinic but you like him—
the way he cradles your asymptomatic son,
explains slowly about developmental milestones
and is so calm he's one valium from unconscious,
and aren't we all addicts to something like the rapture

which will bring both blessing and sorrow? my son
is growing so quickly. i still call him *the baby* but
i put away his small clothes. they go to the crawl space
in boxes labeled with increments of three months, so
isn't childhood like the rapture, if we disappear,
if we flee, if we vanish, we are often missed?

Massive Destruction

Monster Truck Rally (Fishersville, Virginia)

The stadium lights illuminate white clouds of night-sweet
methane—truck exhaust which smells like burning sugar
and hangs over the red bowl of dust where the action is.
Named by the announcer, the trucks roll out one by one:

Spiderman, Grave Digger, Pure Adrenaline. Not trucks, really—
just cages of welded steel and one-hundred-percent engine
with a driver strapped in. A kid in camouflage begs his father
for earplugs when the engines rev. Hats come off for the star-

spangled banner, for the relatives in the service, for the impetus
to fuck shit up, like Iraq, and eardrums, like the line of '70s junkers
in the center of the dirt arena—faithful carcasses of joyrides,
work commutes, and family road trips waiting to be compacted

like so much patient trash. The announcer calls out to folks
watching from the beds of their pickups, dubs them Redneck Hill,
and they cheer when he cracks jokes about taxidermy (redneck
centerpieces) and duct tape (redneck chrome). During intermission

teenage boys gun out on freestyle motorcycles, execute tricks
off a ramp: Cliffhanger, Dead Sailor, and the crowd pleaser:
Kiss of Death, where the rider jacks his legs off the bike
into a handstand, holds a blinking moment midair vertical,

then lets the handlebars go so his bike rides ether and he free-
falls behind, carried forward by Newton to catch his Honda
a split second later and coast down intact—to be fearless
and flying like that, trust physics and touch down unharmed.

Not like the rail-thin boy in the first row caged in a halo-brace
from some real life wreck. His mother threads a yellow slip
of police tape she found on the ground through his brace.
Now the boy reads CAUTION so the crowd won't break him.

The camouflage kid is still pleading for earplugs, blocks
the roaring engines with his own index fingers. His father
ignores his wincing. The crowd roots for Gravedigger crushing
a fresh blue van, sucks a collective breath as the truck leaps in air,

then bounces on rear tires to leave perfect dirt halos which rise,
like offerings, toward the bleachers. Later, in the parking lot,
hemmed in by pickups with confederate flag decals and bumper
stickers that read *God, Guns & Guts* and *Don't Make Me Open*

This Can of Whoop Ass, we will try to remember the whole
makeshift arena filled with red dust and sweetness,
our toughness this delicate, this destroyed.

Interstate Cities

There's no such thing as a singular
lover on the 81 corridor. Our hearts
are large, encompassing flat-bedded
Ferris wheels, ocean-fish containers,
armored cars filled with bills.

I can't recall my pedestrian city—
subway signs vanished and unlit,
directions blotted from gum-pocked
sidewalks, buildings crouched together
in the dark. (*How is your lover*

different?) My love, did I tell you
about the drive home? The limping
car radio, and what grinding sounds
my engine sung: spoons, washboard,
accordion? And you, and you—

hidden in the mountains while each
renegade skateboarder inscribes
Main Street with invisible graffiti,
their wheels etching pavement—
a railing, a parenthetical, a bypass.

(*How is your lover different*
from any other?) My lover's former
lover had a three-legged cat, had a
small studio apartment. One night
he took me to see them. Some cities

resist filling. Some cities resist
skin. At night this city gathers
fog that rolls in like the voice
of a dedication DJ: the wind chimes,
the barren ridge, no lights except

the highway's sodium vapors
and 24-hour motel signs on poles.
The 81 corridor holds every person
in this direction (*app-el-la-shan*)
including the old man

(*cuckold*) who tells the story
about his wife as a bar of soap:
he doesn't mind the others,
as she won't wear out—
or will she? Too many lovers

this town gives up
each winter, turns
inward (they say *empties*).
So how is your lover
like a bar at last call when

each convenience store
is the next brightest place
on earth (*fluorescence*)?
There's nowhere to go
in some cities (*bodies*)

but up, or to the 7-Eleven
parking lot, because why bother
if your lover is not different? If your
city is an exit, if your body
is not inscribed?

You Are Invisible

and everything is tucked in twice.
It is night-time at the Waffle House.
It is night-time and the Food Lion parking lot
is mysteriously full. All our durable goods
roll like marbles down truckers' corridors:
flashes of neon, void intervals, a clock
that doesn't keep time but loses it instead.
Memory vanishes like an inside-out room
shaken over a trash can: the naked space
beneath the bed, the decorative throw pillows,
paste brooches and pockmarked shoes.
You are a city of resin, of negative space,
of chalk. I am the rupture between past
and future, a TV antenna with crosshatched
arms outstretched. I write your name
in new cursive on the condensed glass
of the bus window, erase it with a trace of breath.
The floor here is littered with black gum,
with chicken bones and flattened wrappers.
I am hurtling through transparent distance
beyond which there is no other.
All over town is not that far from here.
I can tell you where to find it.
You can't go into the dark alone.

January Towns

Our bodies are winter clay and we travel
in not-quite-evening—the hour of about-
to-turn, of mistaking a man who owns

the same coat for you. Are you wearing
a red hat? Are someone's arms open
beneath you, her blue apron, her hands

in the air that say *jump*? And the snow
always falling here, always getting swept up.
What number night traveler are you?

There are others: a small girl straddling
a hefty branch, a boy that gazes
at a white-caked statue for luck,

a couple in gray shackled at the ankle—
he eats an apple or speaks into his
cupped hand as if he's on an invisible

CB radio. *Breaker 1-9. Breaker 1-9.*
He tries to pinpoint his location,
but even the pine trees are jet white.

There is a car skidded off the road
with luggage strapped to the roof.
Further back, a pot, a lost shoe,

a hunk of unwrapped Christmas gifts.
We are travelers at dusk in the hallelujah
snow. There is a lone dog humping forward,

a woman with her back to a tree. Maybe
she is me. A couple pushes a house on wheels
through a blizzard. The house tilts

and perhaps it is metaphorical. Perhaps
it is literal. Men in coveralls excavate a well
and a girl rides the train of her own red dress

back up out of its tunnel. Sometimes the light
above the clouds winks out a full-size replica
of our lives. We are crystals of frozen water;

we are hoarfrost situated in the heart of
convenience-store neon, smudged to jeweled
precautions through condensed glass. Home
is the coldest surface where we park our house.

The Violent Legacy of Household Monogamy

Like the ocean of highway whose monoxide breeze
beats the blinds. Like a vestige of something

the last tenants left behind: orphaned wind chimes,
potted plants, the cat that came with the place

ticking softly as a gas meter. It pads around us
while we try, with Band-Aids and conflicted Allen keys,

to assemble the furniture whose sketchy directions
implicate every piece despite the leftover bits

that surround us like the clipped wings of houseflies.
The story I prefer to change-of-address is how a vehicle

took me to a place filled with marzipan doll-fruit
and French appliances: a mistress concealer, a pants-presser,

a tomato-juice gradient. *Take me to your leader*, I insisted,
and the rent-a-cop waved his hands at the entire development,

had a voice like a gravel driveway in an attached house
that crunched with each bounce of the neighbor kid's

basketball, as if he didn't know about the superior qualities
of asphalt. Maybe he really didn't. Every time I mimic

the security guard's pitch, your ears twitch and blister
with joy like I'm performing a magic act that skips

the disappearing objects and sawed halves in favor
of liberating doves from flowers and sticks and hats.

You relocate moths trapped in the house—
call each one *Buddy*, cup its fluttering in your hands

with assurances you'll release it past the screen door.
Your fragile hand-cages predict the plane-catching dreams,

the packing dreams, the bouquets of foxglove and hydrangea
cropping up on my pillow like the locusts in the newspaper

that plagued a Bangladeshi highway, blinding drivers
until dawn when the swarm returned to its agreeable place

and the motorists resumed their journeys. (Home?)
When the angels dressed as moths and doves and locusts

at last decide to blow their trumpets for us, to bless this house,
proximity is a problem. I wash their loudness down the drain,

then remember the song about the spider scaling its way back up.
I don't care if we can't hear them, even faintly. I don't care

if we can't cradle what has been held always, everywhere,
by everybody. I mesh your bandaged fingers with mine.

part two

Ideal
Cities

North Country Canzone

Here in the Adirondacks the last saffron and orange leaves
shade everything in a strange golden light. My mother
writes *be careful of ticks*—to her, any form of nature leaves
open the possibility for disease and alarm—but these leaves
are an innocuous visitation, relics lashed to boughs gone
nearly bare. Two weeks ago I packed the car and left
D.C. the way an explorer in a booby-trapped cave flees
when he hears a specific crack or rolling pebble. The deer
are docile and unflappable here, flicking up their snowy deer
tails when they bend their necks to eat around fallen leaves.
Snowy is a cliché adjective, I know, but I'm pregnant,
the fuzziness and memory-lapse a side effect of this baby,

along with the loose joints and breathlessness of pregnancy.
Even the slowest stroll to the old airplane hangar leaves
me winded. My lungs have less room, claims *The Pregnancy
Book*, to expand, so my body is protesting the baby
by gasping. Aren't all our bodies protesting? My grandmother
turned ninety-four this week, and her left leg is pregnant
with a clot, blocking the circulation. She said that if the baby
kicks in the fourth month, it will be a boy. Her leg will be gone
by next week, amputated. When all the color is gone,
how will it look here? I sit quietly, but I can't feel the baby
moving yet. Without the sun, the leaves are as brown as the deer;
soon the trees will be completely bare. I write a letter that starts, *Dear*

husband, and never send it: *last night I dreamed of white-tailed deer,*
and a trail of blood. I was a failed truck-stop waitress; you left me pregnant
with untranslatable emotion. My grandmother's terms of endearment
for me when she calls are *mein shayna maidel* or *bubbeleh*. The deer
here have *coyach*, the Yiddish word for strength; when they leave
the woods hurriedly, the ground quakes with their heavy deer
bounding, which seems incongruous with their gracefulness. Dear
missing left leg. Dear future child. Your great-grandmother
insisted on the phone that if I looked big at four months, I'd be mother
to a boy. She was high and slurred on hospital Oxycontin. The dear
price of outliving everyone, her silent litany of what's gone
too long to mention, only recited when she weeps over candles on

Shabbos with her eyes covered. I have two hearts, and the second one
beats faster. My anxious dreams. Dr. Sears explains REM, hormones, says *hear*
your dreams—really *listen* and rewrite them with a happy ending. On
my daily walk here I'm often struck with irrational panic—a fear that I've gone
too far, won't have the *coyach* to come back. My mother says this pregnancy
gives Baba strength. I traveled here via Aunt Mary's in Livingston
to see my grandmother before her operation. Aunt Mary drives us in her Lincoln
to Daughters of Israel while Mandy Patinkin croons *Hey, Tsigelekh*. Wet leaves
carpet the Jersey roads in rust; tentlike sukkahs adorned with fruit and leaves
and lights grace each Jewish yard of West Orange. They'll be gone
in a week. They have a sukkah at the rehab center, but my grandmother
refuses to take meals there, says the harvest festival is only for men. My grandmother

is stubborn. She insists on eating in the dining room with her other
table-ladies even though we offer to take her out. Her *coyach* is gone,
she says. The pink and beige room seems filled with every Jewish grandmother
in the tri-state area. Baba immediately sends her diabetic macaroni back; another
grandmother taps me on the shoulder and hands me an album of her dear
grandchildren (*three in Canada—I never get to see them*). My grandmother
has successfully negotiated for waffles instead of herring. Each grandmother
dutifully wears a long white napkin that slips over the head, like a baby's
bib. The ladies at the table that can still hear ask me about my pregnancy
We try to get Baba to eat more, so Aunt Mary tells a long story about my mother
and the hot summer waffles on the boardwalk in Far Rockaway before we leave
Baba to go for dinner. Here, the oaks and beech cling willfully to their last leaves.

O mother of leaves
and sweetness, my grandmother
is not nearly gone.
She is rising like a deer
from the meadow. She is dancing with a baby

                              in her arms.

Christmas Towns

Is it the slotted cardboard box in the post office
for letters to Santa? At 37 weeks you're on the couch
watching a particularly stressful episode of 24, where
Kiefer Sutherland attempts to dismantle something
nuclear and less complicated than the inflatable lawn art
wearing red and white hats across the street—cartoon
characters that tilt in the wind and deflate slowly into a heap
as December progresses. Is it the novelty snow globes?
Your water breaks in the toilet and you haven't packed a bag
for the hospital yet. Is it the felted advent calendar
missing the baby Jesus because the dog ate it? There are
the contractions, the long breaths, the labored drive
along the Potomac, around the Washington Monument.
It is 3 a.m. and the reindeer shells made of lights
duck their heads down to graze on nearly dead grass,
then rise to look at passing cars. This is the only
passing car, and it misses the exit in the dark, obeys
the speed limit and stops a cop for directions. Is it
the staked lawn signs en-route that say *Keep the Christ
in Christmas*? In admissions you repeat your social
security number to a woman behind a keyboard
who smells like cigarettes. You refuse the wheelchair.
They insist. Is it the endless TV loops of women
who get expensive new cars with giant red bows,
or diamonds from mall stores that cause them
to kiss their husbands? You continue to breathe

with no memory of breathing, stand in the shower,
arms draped around your husband—a soaking wet
prom couple slow-dancing. You smooth out brocade
tablecloths, wrestle with shedding garland. Is it
the tether of the fetal monitor? The relief of ice chips
melting on your tongue? Red tail-lights sneak past
the church like marbles in a chute. Is it the summoned
group of nurses leaning near the bed? The mask
over your face? The paralysis? Houses are blanketed
and shut in their winter coats. Is it the exhaustion?
The rolling sensation and drapings? The baby's
heart rate dropping? There are unopened letters
in the North Pole box for Santa. Doorbells and
icicle lights glow carefully on each threshold.
Is it the sheet hung at your neck? The long breaths
and the pulling? Inside each house they celebrate birth.
And then, your son, red and wailing under the heat lamps.

Wound Laced with Evening News, in Which Criss Angel Appears and Vanishes

Secured to my skin an illusionist
is going to heal everything as he
escapes a straitjacket while suspended
over the audience by his ankles in
seconds. (He is particularly stuck, is
painful to remove, is used to support
my body on Oprah invisibly—those
buckles! That hair!). On the news a car
rolling down Constitution sans
driver (the city as asylum) and a baby
in the back (applied in a spiral fashion,
pressed with the thumb); on my body
there will be a slight warming; on my body
(which must be positioned correctly) in order
to apply the lowdown over this area there will be
a slice that looks like a mouthed apple, raised, not like
braille but like the wheel of the bike of the Mormon, who,
when he thought I turned away and wasn't looking popped
a wheelie with white shirt flapping deep to the tune of "That's
Some Buick" (you got there, kid). Have you seen this smile-shaped hole
they pulled someone from (after severe Doppler radar, after car-factory
labor)? Storm Team Seven is waiting at the drop point with all-weather
parkas and windproof hair and other transparent dressing to protect them
from flying debris while the illusionist dislocates his own shoulder (adhesive
border) they pull you up (stuck)—there's no help (as atraumatically as possible)
at the bleeding point gauze is highly absorbent and they count each instrument
to make sure they haven't left one behind, and there's still that car on Constitution
rolling forward at twenty miles an hour with no driver and a baby inside.

Lullaby

Hallelujah, the baby
and I sing everything
all night to put him

to sleep: Oseh Shalom.
California Dreamin'.
Cecilia. Sometimes

The Midnight Special.
We rock and sing
to car alarms,

the silent blue
strobe of cops
cruising our alley,

to the sun-up neighbor
yelling "Freddy"
in a voice that reeks

of methadone and
breakfast. *Let the
midnight special*

the baby and I sing
when the helicopter
circles far-reaching

floodlights through
Southeast for a suspect,
paints the alley with

radiance then moves on
like the ambulance,
like the car chases

the wrong way up
Independence. We are
covered in spit and

sweat and milk. We are
not the only house
with our light on late.

Ideal Cities

Ideal cities are cities where the neighbors
play soul music all night long & don't care

who they bother because who doesn't like Holy Ghost
or Loose Booty? Ideal cities have at least one drunk lady

outside the liquor store mornings, who asks you to hold
her cigarette so she can lean in to touch your baby.

In ideal cities, the pharmacist knows your prescriptions
by heart. In ideal cities your neighbor sells pot to the cops

for a living, though you've never seen him do it & most days
he wears a caftan to glue rhinestones on the cement frogs

in his yard. On trash night in ideal cities your other neighbors
swap stories in the alleys. Ideal cities

have margins that aren't pretty or bleak
and are without proper representation

but have no grievances. My ideal city
has a wish list written on the back

of an envelope scrap, an ATM slip.
My ideal city is peripheral and claims

uneven sidewalks. In the ideal city
my neighbor is a taxi driver.

My neighbor is at sea.
My neighbor thinks

his house is haunted
while his wife's away

on business. My neighbor
gives a robber a glass

of Château Malescot St-Exupéry
and a hug. In the ideal city my neighbors

are a multi-generational
family & one guy

who puts chairs
in the street

to save a spot
for our moving truck.

The Upstairs Notebook

We missed the elephants feeding
on fruit in the stadium parking lot
because it was too difficult to leave
the house today. Most days are
like this now. The circus is in town,

and I am transferring singular objects—
my breast pump, my My Breast Friend
inflatable nursing pillow, my hands-free
pumping bra, my son—from one floor
of our rented row house to another.

This is a many-step process.
This takes longer than orthodontia,
some honeymoons, or a story told
by a kindergartener. The weeping
cherry trees are shedding wet blossoms

outside the door I haven't opened.
I used to watch the front-window
neighbor lovingly wash his tiny blue
hatchback every other day, except
when I had to stop because the car

turned up one morning with a black
trash bag taped over the passenger-side

window and my hormones made me cry.
This is the upstairs notebook.
I have a downstairs one too,

about the neighbor who comes home
from work at five and listens, loud,
to the Bar-Kays' Holy Ghost
in his alley-propped lawn chair.
In my downstairs notebook I also try

to write about the way it feels to walk
with my son strapped to my body,
his wet mouth suctioned to the space
between my breasts. My C-section slash
is still partially numb, and it's raining.

My breast infection is on the mend.
Sometimes my son is sleeping, and today
he sleeps through the idea of elephants milling
a few blocks up, past Dee Dee's Kutz &
Hook-Upz, past the drunks peeing

against the wall of the Mandarin Carry-Out.
In Southeast D.C., a few blocks from us,
there are enormous elephants eating fruit
in the rain, and one day I will tell him
how we almost went to see them.

Miracle Blanket

My mother calls it
that straitjacket.
Do you still put
the baby to sleep
in that straitjacket?
she asks, and I say
Mom, you mean
the miracle blanket?
and she says *yes,*
the straitjacket,
and I have to
admit she's right,
that it looks
like a straitjacket
for babies, especially
in the "natural" color
which resembles a tortilla
so when he's wrapped
the baby seems like a
burrito with a head,
and some nights
the straitjacket
helps him sleep, but
some nights
it does not
though we follow

step-by-step
instructions
and we shush and
swing the baby
wrapped tight
in his straitjacket,
but he screams and
won't go down,
which is what we
call sleep now—
going down, as if he's
drowning in his
straitjacket at 3 a.m.
in our bedroom
and we want him
to drown—we'll do
anything to make him
go down, even pray.
Nicholas of Tolentino,
the patron saint
of babies, is said
to have resurrected
over 100 dead children,
including several
who had drowned
together. He always
told those he helped
to *say nothing of this*.
Holy innocence, my son

in his miracle blanket
is sleeping. O faithful
and glorious martyr,
say nothing of this.

The Chimneys in New Jersey

My mother called to tell me that Esther Blitzer died yesterday, on the 60th anniversary of the liberation of Auschwitz. We ran into her when I was eight at the Galaxy Diner in the Catskills, and it was years before I found out she had buried my grandmother's first daughter in the garden behind the ghetto hospital. My grandmother was a nurse there, Esther was a midwife, and they had both seen the transport women throwing their babies through the bars of cattle car windows. Later, Esther rolled my 70-pound grandmother from the gates of Auschwitz in a wheelbarrow, because she was too weak to run from the Russian soldiers who were raping any women they could find. How could they have greeted each other so normally over rolls and macaroni salad? Some stories are not mine for the telling. Some stories are not humming and breaking with light. They're about chewing with my mouth open, something caught in my teeth. They're about my grandmother harassing the waitress too loudly for more water, then transferring the artificial sweetener from the table to her purse.

My mother said that at the funeral there were chimneys behind the Rabbi's head while he gave the eulogy. *I can't think of the word*, she said. *The chimneys—you know. Industrial. You mean smokestacks?* I said. *Right*, she said. *It was like a poem—bitter cold out and the smokestacks in New Jersey like Auschwitz.* Esther was 90, was history scattered like so much heartwrench and bone. My grandmother is 92, and when she told me to *get married already so I can dance on your wedding*, her *w*'s sounded like *v*'s. *A Jewish wedding is like dancing on Hitler's grave.* She tells me about the card-game regular who was taken to the hospital. No one can say for what, but the poker game broke up and this week my grandmother watches CNN alone in her living room. When I call, there's always a moment when she has to get up and turn it down—the receiver clicking on a table, the blare of someone else's disaster, the shuffle and slap of her house slippers across shag carpet and back before she picks up again to say, *Yest, darling.*

1944

My grandmother made
holes in hand grenades
to leave Bergen-Belsen
each dark night shift—
burnt-out bulbs beneath
the canopy of forest,
bare-shouldered trees
like the thinnest trip-wires,
the name of the unnamed
over and over, hollow
bones scraping the space
nothing could reach.
What would you place
in her outstretched hands?

In the Passport Line

people ask about
my necklace. *Is that
a religious symbol?*

they ask, about these
seed pods sheathed
in resin, a gift from

you, who knows for
what occasion because
now we have a baby

and everything is
muddled. Now we
have a baby who

eats pureed food
and needs a passport
due to my irrational

fear of dictators,
which is no more
or less irrational

than my concern,
for the first months,
that our son would

suffocate on loose
blanket ends, so we'd
put him to sleep

swaddled tight. At night
aren't we all afraid
of suffocating,

and maybe social
networking software or
airplane turbulence?

Some of us dream
of unlaced shoes
under our pillows.

There are many
dark fears. We have
two bedside lamps

for the baby that are
really for us shaped
like shrunken glowing heads:

one blue, one green,
that make our room
a neon aquarium, an

under-the-sea exhibit.
When I went to visit
the jellyfish in Monterey,

I was not married.
We were dating. You were
across the country and I

was with Aimee, who stroked
the starfish in the shallow
Touch-Me Pool without

trepidation. I am not intrepid.
There is a battleship touring
every harbor and I don't wish

to get on it. I am sometimes
claustrophobic. The spy museum
was the only government

exhibit I've wanted to attend—
outdated recorders hidden
in pens and umbrellas,

that car from East Germany
packed with 7 people in the
wheel well alone, someone

wanting to escape so badly
they'd fold themselves for hours
around the engine. My parents

were both refugees and I refuse
religious symbols around
my neck except the loop

of my son's small arms.
With any luck he will never
have to be compact.

Schools of Prophetic Interpretation

Today in the car I was listening to a surreptitious preacher masquerading as a radio comedian. I should have known from the low dial number, the canned laughter, from his über-clean jokes what I had gotten myself into but didn't realize for sure that he was evangelical until he started talking about joy—how happy dogs are to greet their owners and shouldn't we all be that enthusiastic about Jesus?

Sweet Jesus, this is the first year I feel the urge to get one of those electric menorahs for the window—the kind my grandmother used to have, with the orange bulb-flames that you twist-light for each night of Hanukkah. *What will the neighbors think?* When my sister came out, I sent her an ironic postcard that said exactly that, in ornate script, underneath a photo of a creepy family of four looking out a window, curtain pulled back. They are staring at an unspecified scandalous event. They are concerned about the resurrection of the righteous and the wicked.

There was a writer I once met who had to leave his small town after publishing a memoir about his extramarital affairs, though later he repented by finding Jesus and digging wells in South America for the impoverished. There are things I forget and things it is necessary to tell no one. The town never forgave him. I pray a fixed liturgy and we don't have a dog. We often practice joy in the mornings.

If I told my neighbor, Pastor Vince, the things I used to do in Brooklyn, he might not greet me anymore with his gold-toothed smile. His wife would not offer us free rein of her tomatoes. There would be a final judgment, though Vince himself was a heroin addict in the '60s and stabbed someone before he found Jesus. He was penitent and it came to pass. There is scandal everywhere, and I am hoarding the details. You may believe I refuse to be saved.

In Praise of Heat

No one knows the name of the roadside weeds
or the things we pass that shatter: tobacco barns,
waist-high grass, it all rolls out flat and silent
as piecrust on cold marble while fireflies shout
neon in the scrim of trees. I can't find a calendar,
but I'm sure it's August from the boy swinging
his cardboard guitar case on the side of the bypass.
He walked in the relentless morning sun along
a road not made for pedestrians and was not unhappy.
Our hands ride the waves of open-car-window,
which means I can give you a litany of wind-related
directions for solitude but it won't invoke an Airstream
in the rutted dirt of desert, a toaster-as-home.
The desert at night is made of steel and butter.
It is not hot, but full of strumming scrub brush.

We are miles short of the desert, bed down instead
in a strip mall parking lot, consign ourselves
to vinyl and distant howling. There is so much
we left behind: bookshelves, dinner plans,
our neighbors brush-hogging the raspberry patch,
free supermarket samples on a tray. Each piece
of something new is speared with a toothpick,
tucked into crinkled party cups. We will not

eat anything new tonight. We will implement
measures that take into account the open donut shop
a few stoplights back. We will fiddle with each other
while that heat swishes by like the last Cadillac of night.

Pharaoh's Daughter

Like night-swimmers who don't trespass,
won't damage the water they enter,

we were   houses in trees of paperboard
burning slowly; we were

disquieted, hiding
            under tables draped
                    with river willows

from the neighbors
            who howled   like dogs,

from the inflated hall
            of August,   in the cave

of night we were the closest distance;
we were   crickets without end.

Salvation is not to be born again.

Salvation   is a long way down;
I repent often
            by breaking myself
                        and entering.

When the angel Gabriel   appeared
he said, *Lady, night has spit me out.*

This house of wood is blanketed
with leaves, beneath a table which ends
                                        distantly—
a basket boat placed on the sea.

The town sends a virgin to the ocean.
She stands proudly on a ship's prow.

(*All of our service*
was with rigor,   a sacrifice.)

The daughter herself   took the basket,
casket,   arc of bulrushes
daubed with slime and pitch
                    from the water—

wood passages of fallen keys
lowered into her hands
to burn slowly

in the cave of night   we were
                            leaving in torrents,
entering paradise alive
                because I woke   from the dream
where her arm
                was miraculously lengthened—

in the most distant closeness
she was forever   freed from death:
the swollen lobby
      of August;   she was trespassing

and I was with her,
counted forever   among the people

who harness the world,
      not by mortar,
but by shimmer.

A considerable distance from the bank
we trespassed   in the cave of night,

his hands underneath me, in me, and then—

we are burning, we are safe.

I have always been careful
      to identify diagrams of heaven:
tree houses,
    cardboard crates with blankets,
hidden igloos   under tables draped with lace

or basket boats of rushes that float
from arm to arm—

the sacrifice of holding the hand
of the solid, worried god
which raises and empties me (us)

                                  slow, that we are burned

(we were a fire escape
aimed at the moon)

to reach a world   of glitter,
                        not brick.

Pharaoh's daughter and her long arms
harnessed, as if by reins of light—

                        in this most distant closeness
                        take my face in your hands.

Elegy with Construction Sounds, Water, Fish

A nail gun fires into wooden scaffolding up the hill—
the skeleton of a roof unfolding above the trees.
Rat tat tat. Bunk bunk bunk. There is music,
and there is music—the tap of a hammer
smoothing out a mistake. Tall hillside grass
sways, and the houses tucked into the valley
don't do anything. They don't rock
like the black shoulders of mourners.

Something is chirping in the yard,
but in Yiddish the skies are empty
of birds. An air-conditioning unit hums.
The mountains cup the houses the way
a boy might half-moon his hands together
to catch water from a hose that arcs
and splats on cement—skin of water, skin
of pavement. We spend all night outside

staining the deck. The night my grandmother dies
we have to do something. The night my grandmother dies
I dream of my dead friend Chris. He gives me
a fish and I skin it, roll up its white flesh,
secure it with a toothpick on a basement work table.
There is a dearth of fish in Yiddish. In my dream,
Chris and I go out at sunset, roam the streets
of what seems like Queens. He walks off

with his schoolbag slung sideways across his chest
before I can show him the Friday ladies in hats,
the Friday candy store, the whiskered carp slapping
the sides of white bathtubs of my childhood
while my grandmother, bare-armed, wigless,
stands over the kitchen sink with a mallet.
Whatever is chirping in the tall hill grass
won't quit. Yiddish is a world devoid

of trees. My grandmother is dead.
We each took turns burying her
with the rounded side of a shovel,
the sluice of earth sliding over metal.
The dirt hit her wooden box—each clod
and rock. You've heard the sound before.
There is clover in the yard, but Yiddish
has almost no flowers. My aunt will set

a white towel, a pitcher of water
on the stoop. We will wash death
from our hands before we enter her house.
There is music, and there is music.
There is water from a plastic pitcher
hitting slate pavers, silenced by skin.
There are valleys with houses tucked
into them and something trilling

in the grass, and there is Yiddish—
my grandmother's Galicianer accent,
shorthand for a thumping resilient
nameless thing that refuses to leave us,
refuses to sing.

Godspeed

What does a girl do when she discontinues drinking milk?
Each arc of a story is sentient, is pertinent to the final outcome.
My grandmother gives me a *bruchas de kup*. This usually occurs
over the phone. What do you do when you rehearse a play?

These conversations always go the same way: How are you feeling?
I ask, and my grandmother answers, Do you want
I should lie, darling, or do you want I should tell
the truth? Hardships. My grandmother's breath of soup,

of every bathroom cigarette she swore to give up.
What does it mean to replace a book? When we bury
my grandmother, her leg is already in the hole. In the grave.
By Jewish law, Torah scrolls that are damaged beyond use

are shrouded in white and interred like a body. Of blessed memory.
What color is rusty red? It was the '70s and all family photos
have the same patina. They are in a yard in Queens, holding a baby.
The only telltale signs are the arm numbers. They were jobbers,

pieced together hats and sold them to Gimbel's, Lord & Taylor.
They are retired. They are inscribed like books with many pages.
They were solid and inked and holding me. I have never learned
the names of trees. What kind of bark is papery bark?

At a wedding outside Boulder I lean over and ask him,
and he answers, quaking aspen. I love him then,
under the trembling canopy of leaves. What do we mean
when we say the water of the ocean is restless?

The river can turn back. When I break up with a guitarist—
when he leaves me for a girl he meets somewhere outside a bar
in Charlotte, my grandmother calls with lovelorn advice, says,
Could be maybe he was a nice man, but he wasn't for you.

A musician is no good. They cannot live settled in.
You know very well, she says—you a read-up girl.
What does it mean to reread a story? We know the ending
and it's usually OK. We know that everyone is meted out

only as much graceless suffering as they can bear.
What kind of tree is a leafless tree? I send you back,
memory and trembling, I send you back each delicate leaf
of that quaking aspen for one phone call with my grandmother

who will tell me that I didn't bury her, who will tell me
something longer and more important than the pre-assembled
mourning boxes that arrive at the cardboard house today
while we were at the cemetery in Woodbridge, New Jersey,

reciting Psalms with the Rabbi: The sea looked and fled.
Why was it, O sea, that you fled?

Slinky Dirt with Development Hat

O Mama. Juice. Pile of dirt.
Sand pit where the workers stopped
working. Home is a backhoe

with no keys, silent, yellow. Passing
cars buzz the lots for sale that still
have trees, have liens. Our development

is mid-cul-de-sac. There are half-moons
carved into hills, and when we walk
down the unpaved, unnamed road,

past the upright pipes marking gas
or sewer, there's often a father and son
joyriding on one four-wheeler, sans helmets.

They wave hello and we wave back.
There's bankruptcy court. A promised
swimming pool. There's hope that bounces

down the stairs, slinks away, and hides
under a chair. My son pitches a fit
when we pass a digger and I won't stop

for the excavation; when the other children
sing the alphabet, he doesn't join in.
After two servings of milk, there's

water. Farther, further, father.
Mama. Juice. Pile of dirt, he calls
from the car window to the bleached

frames, empty and bowed as a set
of whale ribs, their cupped hands
spilling sand and clay. He presses

his red mitten to the glass and waves
hello to our master-planned community,
the houses that are just like ours, but for

the countertop finish, or optional bonus room
above the garage, or guns in the cupboards
beneath commemorative plates, tucked

next to receipts for winter and re-wear
that coat one more year. In the dusk,
the mountaintops flatten themselves

to escape the calcified bulldozers
that won't come after them anymore.
It is March and there's snow crusted

over with ice. Our jackets are too small,
but the snaps still snap. The zippers still
zip. We shiver and turn up the heat.

May the World to Come Be Neon, Be Water

because my shoes are too tight.
Because I no longer live
in a city of any kind.
Because my husband is asleep,
faceup, in the blue glow of night-light.
Because the crickets are loud
and the shipwreck moon
is right outside the door.
Because it beckons like a torch
I can carry indefinitely through the thicket,
through the meadow. I will furrow

the weeds en route. I will orchestrate
the greatest escape, then come back
so I can tuck a blanket around the baby,
figure out the name of the wildflowers
that bloom purple each morning and vanish
by noon. The windows are open.
I am the only one awake
when the neighbor backs his car
into his own garage door. The bedroom
turns inside out and I smooth the rubric
of his forehead. We will be all right.

Notes

TITLE: The title *Ideal Cities* comes from the work of visual artist Kim Beck (www.idealcities.com).

"NORTH SLOPE BOROUGH": The North Slope Borough encompasses 89,000 square miles of Arctic territory at the top of Alaska.

"WE NEED TO MAKE MUTE THINGS": The line "The world is too noisy, we need to make mute things," comes from sculptor Rachel Harrison's installation for *Collection in Context* (at the Hirshhorn Museum, 2007), where she invented a conversation with the late artist Blinky Palermo.

"POEM WITH/OUT A FACE": Nina Berman's photograph series *Marine Wedding* can be found on her Web site (ninaberman.com).

"AS BOYS GROW (1957)": *As Boys Grow . . .* is the name of a short documentary film from 1957 about the male reproductive system, directed by George Watson and written by Hunter Ingalls, starring the Boys Club of San Francisco.

"The Violent Legacy of Household Monogamy": The Bangladeshi locust incident was taken from a newspaper article entitled "Locusts Plague Highway, Blinding Drivers" (Reuters, May 2, 2005).

"North Country Canzone": The phrase "O mother of leaves and sweetness" is from Sylvia Plath's poem "Winter Trees."

"Ideal Cities": The robbery in this poem is based on the news article, "A Gate-Crasher's Change of Heart," by Allison Klein (*Washington Post*, July 13, 2007).

"Pharaoh's Daughter": The phrase "Lady, night has spit me out" is from the poem "Cry Through the Nights"; the phrases "of glitter, not brick" and "harnessed, as if by reins of light" are from the poem "Evenings in the City." Both of these poems are by Abraham Joshua Heschel, translated from the Yiddish by Morton M. Leifman, from *The Ineffable Name of God: Man* (New York: Continuum, 2005). Special thanks to Basya Schechter (pharaohsdaughter.com).

"Elegy with Construction Sounds, Water, Fish": Some of the lines about Yiddish in this poem come from an analysis of Yiddish vocabulary written in 1943 by Maurice Samuel, as cited by Jonathan Z. Smith in his book *Map Is Not Territory* (Chicago: University of Chicago Press, 1993).

"Godspeed": *"Bruchas de kup"* means "a blessing on your head" in Yiddish. The final two lines are from Psalm 114.

9

The Devil's Hand

Colonel de Crespigny sat stiffly in the *Avenger*'s stern cabin looking around with a mixture of curiosity and distaste.

He said, 'As I have just explained to your, er, captain, I cannot take a risk on such meagre evidence.'

As both the midshipmen made to protest he added hastily, 'I am not saying I disbelieve what you heard, or what you *thought* you heard. But in a court of law, and make no mistake, a man in Sir Henry's position and authority would go to the highest advocates, it would sound less than convincing.'

He leaned towards Dancer, his polished boots creaking on the deck.

'Think of it yourself. A good advocate from London, an experienced assize judge and a biased jury, your word would be the only voice of protest. The schooner's crew can be held upon suspicion, although there is nothing so far to connect them with Sir Henry or any evil purpose. I am certain that fresh evidence will come to hand, but against them, and not the man we are after.'

Hugh Bolitho lay with his shoulders against the cutter's side, his eyes half closed as he said, 'It seems we are in irons.'

The colonel picked up a goblet and filled it carefully before saying, 'If you can discover the village, and some good, strong evidence, then you will have a case. Otherwise you may have to rely on Sir Henry's *support* at any court of enquiry. Cruel and unjust it may be, but you must think of yourselves now.'

Bolitho watched his brother, sharing his sense of defeat and injustice. If Vyvyan was to suspect what they were doing, he might already have put some further plan into motion to disgrace or implicate them. Gloag, who had been invited to the little meeting because of his experience if not for his authority, said gruffly, 'There be a 'undred such villages an' 'amlets within five miles of us, sir. It might take months.'

Hugh Bolitho said harshly, 'By which time the word will have penetrated the admiral's ear and *Avenger* will have been sent elsewhere, no doubt with a new commander!'

De Crespigny nodded. 'Likely so. I have served in the Army for a long while and I am still surprised by the ways of my superiors.'

Hugh Bolitho reached for a goblet and then changed his mind.

'I have made my written report for the admiral, and to the senior officer of Customs and Excise at Penzance. Whiffin, my clerk-in-charge, is making

the copies now. I have sent word to the relatives of
the dead and arranged for the sale of their belongings
within the vessel.' He spread his hands. 'I feel at a
loss as to what else to do.'

Bolitho looked at him closely, seeing him as a far
different person from the confident, sometimes
arrogant brother he had come to expect.

He said, 'We must find the village. Before they
move the muskets and any other booty they've seized
by robbing or wrecking. There must be a clue. There
has to be.'

De Crespigny sighed, 'I agree. But if I send every
man and horse under my command, I'd discover
nothing. The thieves would go to earth like foxes,
and Sir Henry would guess we were on to him. But
"capturing" that wrecker and then exchanging him
was a master-stroke. It would convince any jury, let
alone a Cornish one.'

Dancer exclaimed, 'Sir Henry Vyvyan told you he
knew the prisoner and would catch up with him one
day.'

De Crespigny shook his head. 'If you are right
about Sir Henry, he will have killed that man, or
sent him far away where he can do no harm.'

But Hugh Bolitho snapped, 'No, Mr Dancer has
made the only sort of sense I have heard today.' He
looked about the cabin as if to escape. 'Vyvyan is too
clever, too shrewd to falsify something which could
be checked. If we can find out who the man was, and
where he came from, we may be on our way to suc-
cess!' He seemed to come alive again. 'It is all we
have, for God's sake!'

Gloag nodded with approval. ' 'E'll be from one of Sir 'Enry's farms, I'll bet odds on it.'

Bolitho could feel the flicker of hope moving around the cabin, frail, but better than a minute earlier.

He said, 'We'll send to the house. Ask Hardy. He used to work for Vyvyan before he came to us.'

De Crespigny stared. 'Your head gardener? I'd need a higher trust than that if I had so much in the balance!'

Hugh Bolitho smiled. 'But with respect, sir, you do not. It is my career in the scales, and the good name of my family.'

Avenger rolled lazily at her cable, as if she too was eager to be at sea again, to play her part.

Bolitho asked, 'Well? Shall we try?'

Bill Hardy was an old man whose touch with his plants and flowers was better than his fading eyesight. But he had lived all his life within ten square miles and knew a great deal about everyone. He kept to himself, and Bolitho suspected that his father had taken him on because he was sorry for him, or because Vyvyan had never tried to hide his admiration for and interest in Mrs Bolitho.

Hugh Bolitho said, 'As soon as we can. Carefully though. An alarm now would be a disaster.'

Surprisingly, he allowed his brother and Dancer to return to the house with the mission. To keep it as simple as possible, or to avoid the risk of losing his temper, Bolitho was unsure.

As they hurried across the cobbled square Dancer said breathlessly, 'I am beginning to feel free again! Whatever happens next, I think I am ready for it!'

Midshipman Bolitho and the 'Avenger'

Bolitho looked at him and smiled. They had been looking forward to Christmas together and facing one of Mrs Tremayne's fantastic dinners. But the immediate future, like the grey weather and hint of rain, was less encouraging than it had seemed in *Avenger*'s cabin. It seemed likely they would be facing the table of a court of enquiry rather than Mrs Tremayne's.

Bolitho found his mother in the library writing a letter. One of the many to her husband. There must be a dozen or more at sea at any one time, he thought. Or lying under the seal of some port admiral awaiting his ship's arrival.

She listened to their idea and offered without hesitation. 'I will speak with him.'

'Hugh said no,' Bolitho protested, 'None of us want you implicated.'

She smiled. 'I became implicated when I met your father.' She threw a shawl over her head and added quietly, 'Old Hardy was to be transported to the colonies for stealing fish and food for his family. It had been a bad year, a poor harvest and much illness. In Falmouth alone we had some fifty people die of fever. Old Hardy lost his wife and child. His sacrifice, for he was a proud man, was for nothing.'

Bolitho nodded. Sir Henry Vyvyan could have saved him. But Hardy had made the additional mistake of stealing from him. It was another glimpse of his own father too. The stern, disciplined sea captain, who to please his wife had taken pity on the poor-sighted gardener and brought him here to Falmouth.

Dancer sat down and looked at the fire-place. 'She never fails to amaze me, Dick. I feel I know her better than my own mother!'

She returned within a quarter-hour and sat down at the desk again as if nothing had happened.

'The man's name is Blount, Arthur Blount. He has been in trouble before with the revenue men, but this is the first time he has been taken. He's never in honest work for long, and when he is it is of little value. In and around farms, repairing walls, digging ditches. Nothing for any length of time.'

Bolitho thought of the dead informant, Portlock. Like the man Blount, a scavenger, getting what he could, where he could.

She added, 'My advice is to return to your ship. I'll send word when I hear something.' She reached out and rested her hand on her son's shoulder, searching his face with her eyes as she said, 'But take care. Vyvyan is a very powerful man. Had it been anyone but Martyn here, I might have disbelieved he could do all these terrible things.' She smiled sadly at the fair-haired midshipman and said, 'But now that I know you, I am surprised I did not realize it for myself far earlier! He has links with the Americas and may well have further ambitions there. Force of arms? It is the way he has always lived, so why should he have changed now? It has taken a newcomer like Martyn to reveal him, that is all.'

The midshipmen made their way back to the anchored cutter, feeling the freshening edge to the wind, and noting that several of the smaller fishing boats had already returned to the shelter of Carrick Roads.

Hugh Bolitho listened to their story, then said, 'I have had a bellyful of waiting, but I can see no choice this time.'

Later, when it was dark, and the anchorage alive with tossing white crests, Bolitho heard the watch on deck challenge an approaching boat.

Dancer, who had been in charge of the anchor-watch, clattered down the ladder and struck his head against a deckhead beam without apparently noticing.

He said excitedly, 'It's your mother, Dick!' To the cutter's commander he added in a more sober tone, 'Mrs Bolitho, sir.'

She entered the cabin, her cloak and hair glisten-ing with blown spray. If anything it made her look younger than ever.

She said, 'Old Hardy knows the place, and so should I! You remember the terrible fever I was telling you about? There was some wild talk that it was a punishment for some witchcraft which was being performed in a tiny hamlet to the south of here. A mob dragged two poor women from their homes and burned them at the stake as witches. The wind, drunkenness, or just a mob getting out of hand, nobody really knew what happened, but the flames from the two pyres spread to the cottages, and soon the whole place was a furnace. When the military arrived, it was all over. But most of the people who lived in and around the hamlet believed it was power-ful witchcraft which had destroyed their homes as punishment for what they had done to two of their own.' She shivered. 'It is foolish of course, but simple folk live by simple laws.'

Hugh Bolitho let out a long breath. 'And Blount defied the beliefs and made his home there.' He looked at Dancer. 'And certain others shared his sanctuary, it seems.'

He stepped around his mother, shouting, 'Pass the word for my clerk.' To the others he said, 'I'll send a despatch to de Crespigny. We may need to search a big area.'

Dancer stared at him. 'Are *we* going?'

Hugh Bolitho smiled grimly. 'Aye. If it's another false lead, I need to know it before Vyvyan. And if it's true, I want to be in at the kill.' He lowered his voice and said to his mother, 'You should not have come yourself. You have done enough.'

Whiffin bowed through the door, staring at the woman as if he could not believe his eyes.

'A letter to the commandant at Truro, Whiffin. Then we will need horses and some good men who can ride as well as fight.'

'I have partly dealt with that, Hugh.' His mother watched his surprise with amusement. 'Horses, and three of our own men are on the jetty.'

Gloag said anxiously, 'Bless you, ma'am, I've not been in a saddle since I were a little lad.'

Hugh Bolitho was already buckling on his sword. 'You stay here. This is a young man's game.'

Within half an hour the party had assembled on the jetty. Three farm labourers, Hugh and his mid-shipmen, and six sailors who had sworn they could ide as well as any gentlemen. The latter included the resourceful Robins.

Hugh Bolitho faced them through a growing downpour.

'Keep together, men, and be ready.'

He turned as another rider galloped away into the darkness with the letter for Colonel de Crespigny.

'And if we meet the devils, I want no revenge killings, no *take this for cutting down our friends*. It is justice we need now.' He wheeled his mount on the wet stones. 'So be it!'

Once clear of the town the horses had to slow their pace because of the rain and the treacherous, deeply rutted road. But before long they were met by a solitary horseman, a long musket resting across his saddle like an ancient warrior.

'This way, Mr Hugh, sir.' It was Pendrith, the gamekeeper. 'I got wind of what you was about, sir.' He sounded as if he was grinning. 'Thought you might need a good forester.'

They hurried on in silence. Just the wet drumming of hoofs, the deep panting of horses and riders alike, with an occasional jingle of stirrup or cutlass.

Bolitho thought of his ride with Dancer, when they had joined the witless boy at the cove, with the corpse of Tom Morgan, the revenue man. Was it only weeks and days ago? It seemed like months.

As they drew nearer the burned out village Bolitho remembered something about it. How his mother had scolded him when as a small child he had borrowed a pony and gone there alone but for a dog.